D0988944

Our Version
of the
Antique Original

FOUR LITTLE KITTENS

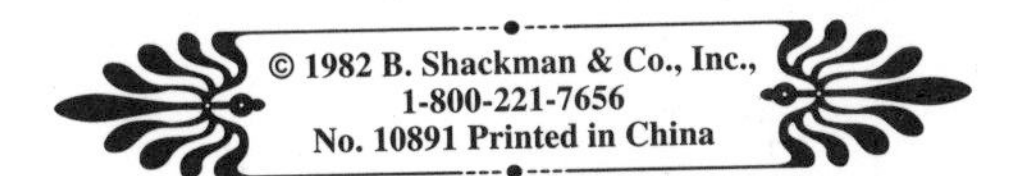

Do You Like Kittens ?

Do You Love Kittens ?

Once upon a time there were four little kittens. Their names were Buzz, Fuzz, Suzz, and Agamemnon.

Their mother's name was Samantha. She taught her four little kittens to say *please.* She taught them to say *thank you.* She taught them their purring lessons. And she taught them always to wash behind their ears.

When Fuzz was extra good, her mother gave her cream for breakfast.

When Suzz was extra good, her mother let her make a gingerbread man with catnip eyes.

When Buzz and Agamemnon were extra good, their mother let them dress up and play pirate.

And when her four little kittens were *all* extra good, Samantha let them go out with their friend Toodles on a hayrack ride.

Agamemnon had the hardest time to be extra good. He was the youngest and sometimes he forgot. Sometimes he even got into the jam pot.

JAM

Then, of course, Samantha had to send that naughty kitten straight to bed.

Every day, except Saturday and Sunday, Buzz and Fuzz and Suzz and Agamemnon all put their spelling books and their A-B-C books into their little red bags and scampered off to school.

SCHOOL
SPELLING
A B C
SPELLING

Buzz, Fuzz, Suzz, and Agamemnon already knew how to spell C-A-T and R-A-T for Miss Simpkins, their dear teacher.

Cat Rat
2X2=4
2X4=8
5
3
8
4X4=16
2X3=6
ABCDEFGHIJKL
SPELLING BOOK

Buzz, Fuzz, and Suzz were good little kittens. But Agamemnon was the youngest, and sometimes he forgot the rules. Sometimes he laughed when his friend Toodles made a funny face. Then they both had to wear dunce caps until they were sorry.

DUNCE
DUNCE

One Saturday morning Samantha went out shopping. Then Buzz, Fuzz, Suzz, and Agamemnon went to the brook. It was their mother's birthday, and they wanted to catch her a present.

Agamemnon waved his fishhook, but only caught the seat of his pants.

Buzz and Fuzz and Suzz did not catch any fish at all. But after a while Agamemnon caught one, and Suzz said he was a very smart kitten.

On the way home Agamemnon gave Fuzz a ride in his little wooden cart.

Buzz, Fuzz, and Suzz then put on their cooking caps and aprons and made their mother some catnip birthday cakes all by themselves.

Then Buzz caught a birthday mouse for his mother. Fuzz lifted her skirts, and was not sure she liked that present!

After that, Suzz and Agamemnon went out to the barn, and hunted for nice fresh eggs that Mrs. Hen and the Cackle sisters had just laid. They wanted them, too, for the birthday supper.

At last their mother came home. The four little kittens ran to her, singing,

Happy Birthday! Mew! Mew!
Happy Birthday! Mew! Mew!
Happy Birthday, dear Mother,
Happy Birthday! Mew! Mew!

Then they gave her the fish and the eggs and the mouse, and plenty of kisses on her whiskers.

And then Fuzz brought in the catnip birthday cake she had made. Samantha was so happy!

After the birthday supper, she said, "You were all such extra good kittens—even Agamemnon—that I am going to take you to the Kitten Fair tonight. I feel like celebrating, myself."

First they washed and wiped all the supper dishes. Or anyway, they helped, while Suzz did most of the work.

Then they all washed behind their ears and went to the Fair. And the first thing they saw there was a kitten clown with a funny hat. They all laughed and clapped their paws hard.

Next they went to the rummage sale and bought lots of jam. And Buzz thought he liked *that* best.

RUMMAGE SALE
JAM

Then they all took turns sliding down a slide on a sled. Agamemnon fell off. And Agamemnon thought he liked *that* best.

Fuzz saw a very nice movie show, and Fuzz thought she liked *that* best.

Suzz liked swinging on a swing. So did Agamemnon. But Agamemnon remembered "ladies first," and gave Suzz the first swing. And Suzz thought she liked *that* best.

The very last thing that Buzz and Fuzz and Suzz and Agamemnon and their mother did was to eat a picnic supper. And they all *knew* they liked *that* best.

That night the four little kittens kissed their mother, and thanked her for the lovely time they had had at the Kitten Fair. And she thanked them again for their birthday presents, and for being so very good.

But when she tucked Agamemnon into bed, Samantha remembered he was the youngest and had tried the hardest. So she gave him an extra kiss on the tip of his nose.

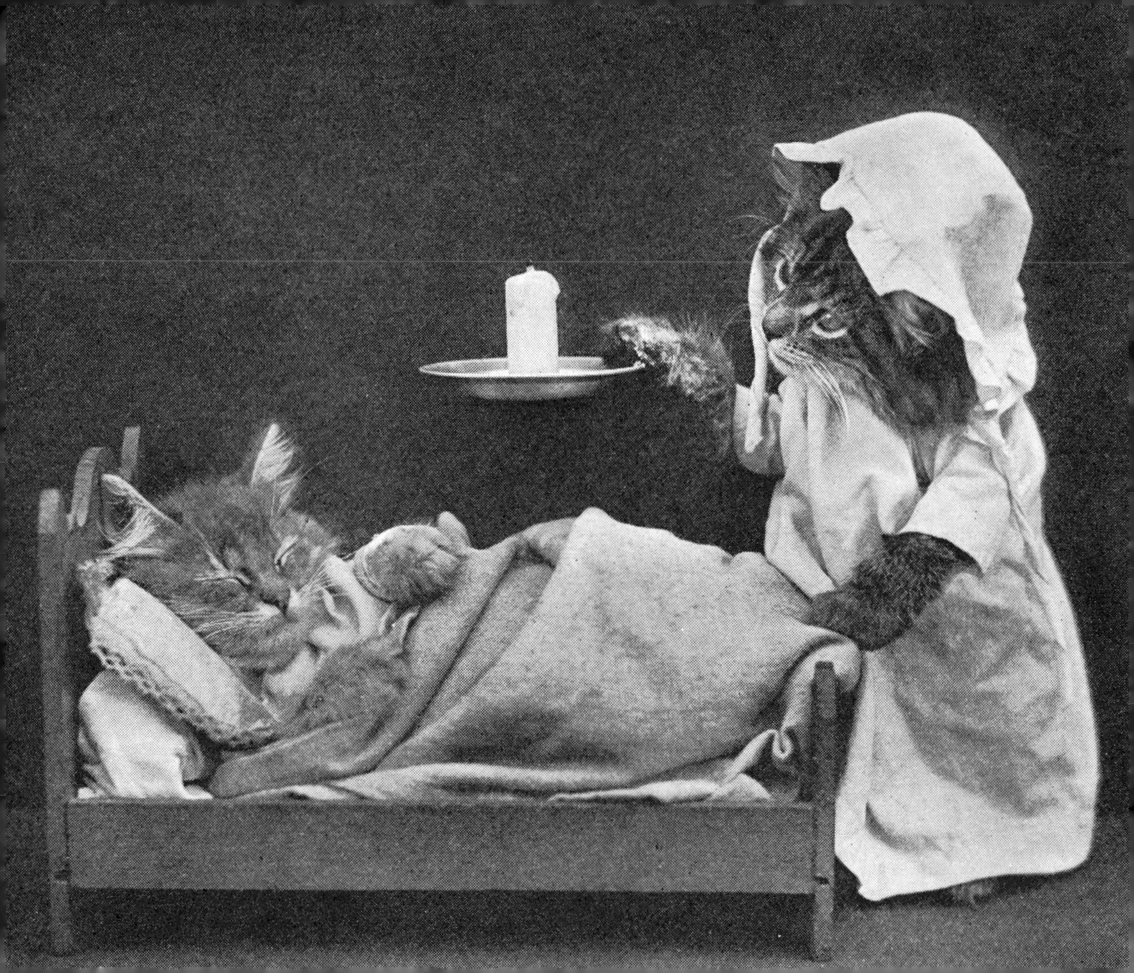

Did You Enjoy
This Story ?
Good !
Now Go To Sleep